Number Six

Dorling Kinderlsey
www.dk.com

Editor Fiona Munro
Designer Lisa Hollis

Published in Great Britain in 1997
by Dorling Kindersley Limited, 9 Henrietta St, London WC2E 8PS
This edition published in 2000

A CIP catalogue record for this book is available from the British Library.

ISBN 0-7513-6706-0

Color reproduction by DOT Gradations
Printed in Hong Kong by Wing King Tong

Number Six

COLIN AND JACQUI HAWKINS

Dorling Kindersley

"I love to play tricks!" said Number Six.

Hi!

Number Six lived in a cosy house with a bright yellow roof, six pink chimney-pots and six windows. It was the sixth house in Numbertown. The address was 6, Number Lane. "It's magic!" he said.

Number Six was a magician.
He had lots of magical things in his house.

Six top hats,

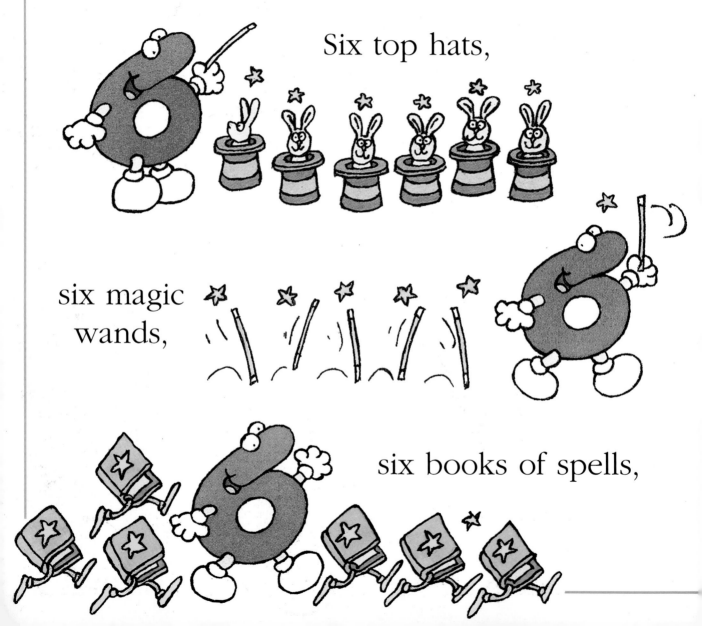

six magic wands,

six books of spells,

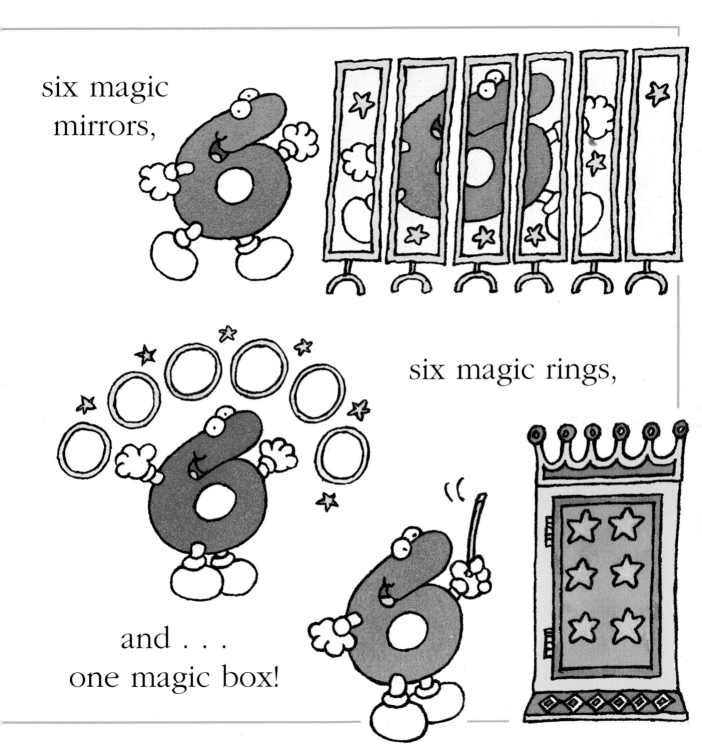

six magic
mirrors,

six magic rings,

and . . .
one magic box!

Watch this!

"Watch this trick!"
said Number Six.
He tapped the magic
box six times with his
magic wand and out
flew six white doves!

"Coo! Coo! Coo!
Coo! Coo! Coo!"

"It works like magic," laughed Number Six.

The birds flew round and round the room
six times, until Number Six was quite dizzy.

Yawn!

The next morning, Number Six woke up at six o'clock. He yawned six yawns, got out of bed, and tapped the magic box with his magic wand.

Tap! Tap! Tap!
Tap! Tap! Tap!

Number Six was amazed. Instead of six white doves, out hopped six white rabbits. They hopped six hops and were gone!

"They've hopped it!" he said.

"Where have those rabbits got to?" puffed Number Six, as he chased after them. He found the six naughty nibblers busy munching a field full of juicy carrots.

Chomp! Chomp! Chomp! Chomp! Chomp! Chomp!

"We're hungry!" they said, as Number Six looked at the empty field in horror.

Who's playing tricks
on Number Six?

"Oh rats!" said Number Six,
as he waved his magic wand
six times over the six giggling rabbits.

"That's right," squealed six white rats.
"We're Tatty, Matty, Patty,
Hatty, Batty and Fatty,"
they squeaked before scampering off.

Who's playing tricks
on Number Six?

"What a rat race!" gasped Number Six,
as he ran all over Numbertown
looking for them.
"I give up," said Number Six at last,
and he went home.

He found the six rats in his kitchen.
"Yummy cakes," said Hatty.
"Don't talk with your mouth full," said Tatty.
They all sniggered and
blew crumbs over Number Six.

"Oh crumbs!" cried Number Six, and he waved his wand six times over the rats.

ZAP! ZAP!
ZAP! ZAP!
ZAP! ZAP!

The rats disappeared, and six huge cakes lurched towards Number Six. "We want to eat you up," they giggled. "You're so sweet." Number Six was horrified. The cakes got closer and closer.

Who's playing tricks on Number Six?

As he ran, Number Six shook six specks
of magic dust over himself.

ZAP! ZAP! ZAP!
ZAP! ZAP! ZAP!

Six seconds later, he woke up.
It was six o'clock, and Number Six was
safe and snug in his own little bed.
"Thank goodness.
It must have been a bad dream," he said.

"I hope that really was a dream,"
said Number Six, as he gently tapped the
magic box six times with his magic wand.
Out flew six white doves.

"I love to play tricks!"
said Number Six.

"Sweet dreams," the doves cooed.
"That's magic!" laughed Number Six.